Moomin
and the Magic Hat

Moomin and his Friends

Sniff

Moominmamma

Moomin

Moominpappa

The Hemulen

Snork

The Snork
Maiden

Little My

Snufkin

Moomin
and the Magic Hat

Tove Jansson

HEINEMANN · LONDON

Spring had arrived in Moomin Valley.
Moominhouse was no longer covered
with snow and the sunshine had woken
everyone up after their long winter's
sleep.

Moomin flung open his window.

"Wake up, everyone!" he yelled. "It's
spring!"

Little My was not happy. She was having a lovely dream, and did not want to be woken up.

"Good spring, everyone!" said Moominmamma.

"I'm starving," cried Little My.

"Don't worry," said Moominmamma. "We can all have a nice big breakfast."

In the distance Moomin could hear Snufkin, playing a tune on his mouth organ.

Snufkin and Moomin decided to wake up Sniff, and then do something really exciting.

"I can think of much more exciting things to do than this," complained Sniff, as they huffed and puffed to the top of a mountain.

"Maybe we're the first ever to climb this mountain," suggested Moomin. "Look at the view!"

Suddenly, Moomin spotted a large top hat behind a stone.

Moomin took the hat home.

"Look at this nice top hat we found, Pappa," he said. "We brought it back for you."

Moominpappa decided to try it on.

"Hmm. It's much too big for me," he grunted. "Whoops! I can almost get right inside it!"

Moominpappa tried to get the hat off, but it was stuck.

Moomin pulled harder and harder, until *pop!* at last it came off.

"It's a very smart hat," said Moominmamma.

"I think there's something strange about it," said Moominpappa.

But Moominmamma had already decided what to do with it.

"It's a waste-paper basket," chuckled Sniff.

Moominpappa put some paper into the hat. All of a sudden it started to grow bigger... and bigger...

Moominpappa couldn't believe his eyes.

A few moments later, a fluffy pink cloud came out from the hat, and floated out of the house and into the garden.

"Oooh!" said Sniff.

"Gosh!" cried the Snork Maiden.

Lots of pink clouds had appeared and they felt like cotton wool. Moomin jumped on top of one.

"This is wonderful," he shouted. "I'm floating!"

"Don't go too high. You might fall off," warned Sniff.

Soon all the children were flying about on the clouds.

But after a while the clouds started to break up and, one by one, everyone fell to the ground.

"That was great fun!" said Snufkin.

"I don't want to stop," moaned Little My.

Later that day, the children played hide-and-seek. Sniff counted to ten.

Moomin looked for somewhere to hide. Then he found the perfect place. Yes! Inside the hat!

"Coming!" called Sniff, as he ran to find his friends.

Sniff soon found everyone. Only Moomin was missing.

"Haven't you found him yet?" asked the Snork Maiden, anxiously.

All of a sudden, they heard a laugh coming from inside the hat. A strange creature climbed out and said: "Here I am, Sniff!"

"Ha ha! I've won! You couldn't find me," giggled Moomin.

"Who would want to find *you*?" asked Little My.

The others had no idea who this ugly creature was. Moomin looked like some kind of monster.

Moomin looked at himself in the mirror. "Oh no!" he gasped. "What is this horrible thing with a bushy tail...it *can't* be me!''

Poor Moomin rushed up to Moominmamma.

"Mamma," he cried. "Please believe me. I *am* Moomin."

"Well you don't look like my Moomin," replied Moominmamma.

Moomin begged her to believe him and tears came into his eyes.

Eventually, Moominmamma realised this strange creature was indeed her little Moomin.

Without any warning, Moomin suddenly changed back to his usual shape.

"Oh Mamma!" cried Moomin.

Everyone laughed with joy to see the Moomin they knew so well.

"You're right, Pappa," said Moominmamma. "There is definitely something dangerous about that hat."

Moominpappa decided that they should not keep
the hat any longer, and Moomin threw it in the river.
He and Snufkin watched it float slowly away.

It *was* rather a special hat, wasn't it?

Moomin Valley

Adapted from *Finn Family Moomintroll* by Tove Jansson
Copyright © 1948 Tove Jansson

This edition first published in Great Britain in 1993
by Heinemann Young Books
an imprint of Reed Consumer Books Limited
Michelin House, 81 Fulham Road, London SW3 6RB
and Auckland, Melbourne, Singapore and Toronto
Text copyright © 1993 by Reed International Books Limited
Illustrations and cartoon adaptation copyright
© 1993 Moomin Characters/Bulls/Telecable Benelux bv
Exclusively licensed by Telescreen International bv

ISBN 0 434 96247 3

A CIP catalogue record for this book is available at the British Library

Printed in Italy by Olivotto